Samuel J. Margolin,
lovingly remembered

First Edition

*Published simultaneously in Canada
by Little, Brown & Company (Canada) Limited*

Printed in Singapore for Harriet Ziefert, Inc.

I Won't Go To Bed!

BY

HARRIET ZIEFERT

ILLUSTRATED BY

ANDREA BARUFFI

LITTLE, BROWN AND COMPANY
BOSTON   TORONTO

It was time for small boys to be in bed.
But Harry folded his arms and said,
"I won't go to bed. I won't. I won't."

"Then don't," said Harry's father.
And up the stairs he went.

Harry said, "I'm going to stay up all night."

He sat himself in his father's chair.

He looked at the newspaper, then
he switched the television on and off.

Harry found a good spot on the floor.
In the quiet of the night he listened
to the steady sound of his father breathing.

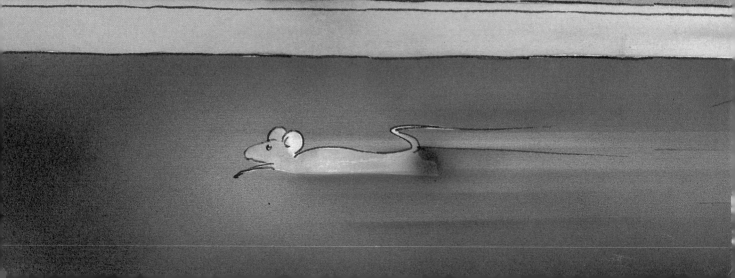

At 12 o'clock a mouse dashed across the room.

At one o'clock an owl hooted. Whoooo!
Shadows moved along the wall.
A window rattled.
Harry shivered—just a bit.

The clock said two.

The mouse ran back across the room
and looked at Harry as if to ask,
"Why aren't you in bed?"

"I won't go to bed. I won't,"
repeated Harry.
"Instead, I'll have a party!"

Harry put a blanket on the floor.
He set places for two guests.

Harry sat at the head of the table.
He wished he could begin the party.

But no one came.
Not even the mouse.

"So what," thought Harry. "I'll sing."

Harry only sang a few notes, for
his voice sounded loud and strange
against the quiet of the night.

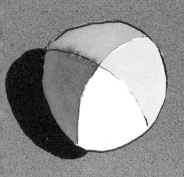

Harry was lonely and tired.
He curled up to take a little rest.

It was five o'clock.
Night was turning into day.
Harry's father came down the stairs.

He kneeled and asked, "Harry, would you like to go upstairs to bed?"

Harry sat up slowly and nodded yes.

Harry held his father's hand.
Together they climbed the stairs.